Complicated Simplicity

By

Kaylynn Hunt

Published by Skylar Publications

www.KaylynnHunt.com

Kaylynn@KaylynnHunt.com

This novel is strictly fictional. All characters, places and events are from the author's imagination and/or used fictitiously. Any resemblances to business establishments, actual events, locales or persons dead or alive are completely coincidental.

Complicated Simplicity by Kaylynn Hunt.

Cover Design: Qunair Jones

https://www.instagram.com/tattooguy_q

All Rights reserved. This book in whole or part shall not be reproduced without expressed written consent of author.

Dedicated to:

Mr.

Thank you for making me see love everywhere, for making me feel as if there is no other love like ours.

&

The Lady

Giving you something to read was the catalyst for me to step outside my norm allowing me the opportunity to explore an avenue that exceeded even my expectations.

Note to readers:

For those of you familiar with my work. This is something different. You can still expect my normal surprise twists and unthought-of revelations but this will be something different.

I will say; this is my proudest piece of literature. The depth of emotion in these words were previously untouched. I hope you enjoy this little tale.

Serenity

Serenity stood in the mirror admiring the dress she wore. Her mother and grandmother stood on either side of her while Aunt Lillian sat in a chair behind them. Even she noticed the glow that enveloped Serenity.

"You look absolutely beautiful," her mother proclaimed.

"I know mother. It is nice, isn't it?"

"It's about time you showed off what your mamma gave you," Aunt Lilly yelled from her chair.

Lillian was the liveliest of the bunch. She was always loud and boisterous. No one could ever accuse her of not speaking her mind. But she was also soulful, loving and surprisingly compassionate. Lillian and Lydia were two polar opposites and sometimes didn't like one another but, they stuck together. Lydia and Lillian were born an hour apart; they were like day and night, literally. Lydia was a plump, round-faced, chocolate coated, short hair wearing nerd. Lillian on the other hand was a slim built, heart shaped face, tan skinned, long haired wild child.

"Hush Lillian, it ain't for everyone to see," Lydia said.

"I think you always look beautiful baby," her grandmother stated.

Mammie was a quiet woman who spoke as if she was singing most of the time. Her words were melodic and if you listened to her speak long enough you may think she'd sang you a lullaby. Lillian and Lydia were her only children and Serenity her only grandchild. She wasn't a particularly large woman and she always seemed to have a smile on her face. Growing up,

Serenity never saw her angry but for some reason everyone was afraid of her.

There was a knock at the door.

"You ready in there, Smooch?" Her dad asked on the other side of the door.

"Yes daddy, I'm just about ready."

"I wish he would just go away," Aunt Lilly said in a hushed tone.

"Be nice, Aunt Lilly," Serenity stated.

"I said it quiet. That is nice."

Lillian didn't say all the things she really wanted. She couldn't stand Harold from the day she'd met him. Sometimes, she thought Lydia just went out with him to piss her off. He was as slick as a banana peel. Lilly never trusted him. For her, he wasn't good enough for her sister. But Lydia always thought Lilly was just jealous and wanted him for herself. Back then, they were always in competition. There was no way she would have let him go, just to prove Lillian wrong.

But Harold was just as Lillian thought. He was a slick talking, smile toting, scheming, conniving ladies' man. Who wouldn't stand up and fight for her sister when she needed it most. That was the one time she hated to be right. Lillian couldn't deny the beautiful life they created was the light of her life. Though Lillian never had children of her own, she felt as if Serenity belonged to her just the same.

Serenity usually hid behind her hair. Today, it was pulled away from her face with big luxurious curls. Her face was made up just enough to bring out her eyes which were doe like. The necklace she wore had been passed down to her from her grandmother (something old). As she stood in the mirror watching her mother and aunt bicker behind her she thought of the day she met, Baxter.

A year ago.......

He'd walked into the bookstore without Serenity noticing. She was seated in her usual spot near the window, in her favorite chair. Serenity's cup of tea was on the round table in front of her as usual. There was another chair adjacent to her which remained empty, as always. Suddenly, she was jarred from her book by a sultry baritone voice.

"Is there anyone sitting here?"

Serenity was confused; no one ever spoke to her. She looked up from her book, slowly. At first, she was speechless. *Was he real?* Her eyes had to be deceiving her. He repeated as he motioned to the empty chair.

"Is there anyone sitting here?"

"No," she said as she shook her head then immediately went back to her book.

"Do you mind if I sit?"

Without returning his gaze or saying a word she shook her head, again. Baxter sat in the adjacent chair, placing his cup on the opposite side of the table. Serenity pretended to continue to read. But, she couldn't stop thinking about the face she'd just seen. His neatly trimmed beard was the first thing that caught her attention. In the short-time she searched his face; there wasn't a visible scar or blemish, his skin looked as smooth as butter. Those eyes that searched hers for an answer were so hypnotizing and his **teeth** straight, pearly white. *He couldn't be real.* Serenity got a quick glance at his hand, no ring. He was dressed nicely, businessman like. Trying to inconspicuously get a better look at him; Serenity reached for her tea then sat back to take a few sips. He glanced at her over his paper. She quickly went back to pretending to read. With her head lowered and her long, bushy, curly hair covering her face, she leaned forward to place her cup back. Missing the edge of the table her cup tipped over, the remainder of its contents spilled. Immediately, Serenity jumped from her seat.

"Oh my God! I'm so sorry," she said as she hurried to place a napkin over the spill.

"It's ok," he said as he grabbed his cup from the table so it wouldn't get wet.

"I'm so clumsy."

"Nonsense, everything happens for a reason."

"Sure, there's a reason to spill tea on the table," she said sarcastically.

"I bet I can find several reasons."

Serenity continued to blot the tea with a few napkins then went to retrieve more to continue cleaning her spilled mess, without responding to his last statement. She began thinking of the reason she picked that cold ass tea up in the first place. He began to chuckle and she looked at him out the corner of her eye.

"Is something funny?"

"No, I was just thinking to myself. Let me get you another tea."

"That's not necessary."

"Sure, it is. Maybe that's the reason you spilled the tea. Simply, so I could buy you another," he said and walked away before she could protest again.

When he stood, Serenity couldn't help but watch him walk away. She took in his broad shoulders, bow legs and the sway in his steps. Shortly after, he returned handing her a cup with fresh steam spilling from its top. She accepted but something strange happened when her hand touched his. Serenity could've sworn she'd seen a beam of light shine down on him. Quickly, she shook her head, blinked then looked at him again. He noticed the perplexed look on her face.

"Is there something wrong?" He asked.

"No, nothing's wrong. There was just a glare maybe reflecting from the door or something. I'm fine."

Instinctively, she sniffed to get a nose full of the aroma coming from her cup.

"How did you know what I drink?"

"I'm psychic," he said with a smile.

"You shouldn't joke about things like that," she said straight faced.

"Who says I'm joking? I bet I know your name."

"Tell me then."

"Let's see. I'm feeling something calm. Starts with," he paused.

"Starts with annnnnnnnn S. Am I right so far?"

"Go on."

"Sara, Sasha, Stacy, no Serenity. That is your name, isn't it?"

"Yes, that's it. How'd you know?" She asked with a look full of skepticism.

"I told you, I'm psychic. My name is Baxter by the way," he said as he extended his hand.

"Nice to meet you Baxter, but I'm still not convinced."

He'd taken his seat again across from her and she hadn't picked her book up. She peered over her cup as she sipped her tea, taking him in. Serenity studied his facial expressions. It amused her the way he attempted to give exaggerated gestures of him trying to guess her name. There was a hint of a smirk on her face as she reached across the table to meet his outstretched hand. She was almost scared to touch him again after what happened the last time. His large, strong hand engulfed her dainty phalanges. The sky didn't open up and rain light down on them. So, she dismissed the thought that the light was ever real the first time.

Baxter glanced at his watch.

"Well, it was nice buying you tea. I'm sure we'll see each other again, Serenity. Enjoy your day."

"Thank you, Baxter. You enjoy your day as well."

Just like that he was gone.

Serenity went back to her book but her mind was now restless.

Why didn't I say something else? Who am I kidding? He'd never want to go out with someone like me.

She wouldn't even allow herself to fantasize about the possibility. But, she couldn't wait to get home to tell Janice about him.

Janice will get a kick out of this. I must be crazier than everyone else thinks.

She chuckled then dismissed the whole idea of Baxter ever having any interest in her.

Baxter

"Will you stop pacing?" Clayton said.

"I can't help it."

"Baxter, what are you worried about?"

"I'm more anxious than worried, I guess," Baxter said as he sat down.

"Well, calm your ass down. You're making me nervous."

"I just can't wait to see her come down that aisle," he said and jumped back out of his seat.

"What if she changed her mind?" Baxter asked.

"Man, why would she want to do that?"

Clayton was Baxter's best friend, brother, now best man and only groomsman. He couldn't remember ever seeing Baxter act like this. He was always so confident and assured. Today, he seemed scattered and kind of afraid.

"There's no telling what is going through that brain of hers."

"I'm sure, she's anxious to get to you."

"Distract me. Did you get rid of that last girl I saw you with?"

"Shelia? I'm fucking trying. She won't go the fuck away."

"We are in a church, Clay."

"Oh. Sorry, Lord. Hell, what am I apologizing for He knows how much I curse. Church ain't the only place He can hear me."

"Can you just try to tone it down?"

"Like I was saying, she keeps popping up."

"I told you, I don't like her. She's not good for you. Cut her off. You know I'm never wrong."

"I know, I know. But the sex is off the chain."

"Contrary to what you believe, there's more to life than sex. She's bad news."

"Just because you're marrying the woman of your dreams doesn't mean I want to even meet mine yet."

"I'm not talking about you settling down. You're not ready for that, yet. But that girl is NO good. Find someone else to sex."

"Alright man, I trust you. I'll leave her be."

Baxter didn't believe him. He knew Clayton better than anyone and he knew he'd go back for one last hurrah. The moment he'd seen Sheila; Baxter knew she was not good for anyone. She was dark and devious. Clayton would be caught up in no time if he didn't take heed to what he was being told this time.

"Is Trista coming?"

"Of course, she's probably out there waiting."

Clayton gave his brother a side eye. He knew him all too well. Trista was a neighbor turned longtime friend of them both.

Baxter had been pushing for him to get with Trista for the longest. Lately, he hadn't said much about it but he knew what he was thinking by even his mention of her.

"Hey did I ever tell you about the first time I saw Serenity?" Baxter asked interrupting Clay's thoughts.

"Man, I've heard that coffee story a million times. PLEASE don't tell it again."

"That's not the first time I saw her and it was tea. That was the first time she saw me."

"What do you mean? Don't tell me you're a stalker, dude."

"Ha! I guess I am."

"You are like totally blowing my mind," Clay said in his weak attempt at a valley girl voice.

As Baxter thought about that day he first saw Serenity, he zoned out for a minute. He was on his way to a business meeting in a suburban area just outside of Detroit. As he ran across the street he was stopped dead in his tracks. At first, he just got a glimpse of her from the corner of his eye. It happened to be raining that day but, for some reason it seemed as if the sun had just brightened only for him. When he turned to get a full view of what had been playing in his peripheral, his steps were halted. There he stood in the center of Main Street, no longer shielding his head with his trench coat, staring at a rainbow in the distance. She was standing at the door of a bookstore. Seemingly, deciding if she would battle the rain drops. Her hair looked like a lion's mane but was somehow just right. Her skin looked as smooth as a sheet of paper but the color of a paper bag.

Baxter nearly needed to squint because of the bright colors that surrounded her. He'd never seen colors so bright or vibrant. Usually, he saw one, two, maybe even three colors but with her it was indeterminate. Every color in the rainbow and all the ones in between filled his eyes. From where she stood, not even aware of his gaze, he could feel the warmth that radiated from her soul. He could tell her spirit was the purest he'd ever seen. He had to meet her; he had to see what her rainbow consisted of.

"HELLO! Earth to B," Clay said snapping his fingers in Baxter's face.

"Sorry, dude."

"Sooooo, are you going to tell me or what?"

"She was coming out of the bookstore as I was crossing the street. I almost got hit by a car. Her beauty stopped me in my tracks. I was standing in the middle of the street like a damn fool."

"The same store you met her?"

"Yes, I went back a week later hoping she'd be there again."

"Stalk-er!"

"Hey! It paid off."

"I guess it did."

"That was the best decision I ever made. It nagged at me for days. If she wouldn't have been there, I would have gone back every day."

"You do know you sound like a crazy person?"

"Love will make you do crazy things."

"You hadn't even met; you didn't know you loved her."

"Haven't you ever heard of love at first sight?"

"That doesn't mean I believe it."

"I don't care. She intrigued me, without even noticing me."

"So, tell me, how DID you know her name?"

"That's easy, it was on her cup. And I knew what she was drinking because I asked the barista."

"Slick man, slick."

"I'm resourceful. But, I'm sure she figured it out, she never let on."

"You're still a stalker."

"I'm a man that goes after what he wants."

"If you say so. You ready for tonight? Is that why you're so nervous?"

"Am I ready? Shiiiiii…. I mean shoot. I've been ready."

"I can't believe you guys have never had sex. I don't think I could do that."

"I'm not going to say it was easy. I know it will be worth the wait."

"What if she's horrible at it? I mean; I've had some bad pussy."

"Language!"

"Oh, sorry, there is such a thing as bad sex. What will you do if it's just BAD?"

"It won't be. It'll be spiritual, phenomenal."

"If you say so dude," Clay conceded, though he was not convinced.

"Ye of little faith, you should try connecting with someone's heart, mind, and soul before you plug into their bodies. You'd be surprised."

"I'll stick with plugging in first and letting the rest follow. But, like you said, I'm not ready for all that."

Serenity

For some reason, as she stood preparing to meet her man at the altar, Serenity began thinking about her first boyfriend. When she met him, she wouldn't give him the time of day. Just like with Baxter, she couldn't believe he was talking to her. Her self-esteem needed a lot to be desired, in high school it was less than existent.

She was the new quiet nerd and didn't want to fit in with the jocks, socialites or mean girls. All Serenity wanted was to be left alone. Being forced to move to some place miles away from where she'd known all her life, in her senior year was enough reason for her to be angry with life. Not to mention, what brought her there in the first place. Being noticed by the starting safety on the football team was the last thing on her mind.

The day Trenton first spoke to Serenity was not a great day for her at all. She just wasn't in a good mood but he was waiting as she walked out of class. She had no idea he'd been waiting for her until he ran behind her, after she refused to acknowledge him standing in front of the locker next to hers.

He'd been watching as the calculus teacher returned last week's quizzes and noticed the 100% on the top of hers. While he looked down at his 55%. Trenton had the bright idea of getting to know the new girl.

"Your name is Serenity, right?" He asked, startling her as he came to a stop next to her.

"Yes," she said apprehensively, wondering what he wanted with her.

"I'm Trenton."

"I know who you are."

"Well, I noticed your quiz score and I was wondering if you'd be interested in tutoring me."

"No," she said without breaking stride then continued to her next class as if he meant nothing.

Trenton stopped walking and watched her back in disbelief. He wasn't used to the girls telling him no. Trenton wasn't prepared for her response and was at a loss for words. Serenity dismissed his request as soon as it was asked assuming it was just his usually ploy to attempt to get in her jeans, which wasn't happening. She thought more about it when she got home and came to the conclusion that he just wanted her to do his homework for him or something. As she sat in her room thinking about the nerve he had, her father knocked at her door.

"Yes, daddy."

"There's a boy here to see you."

"What? Who?"

"He says his name is Trenton."

Serenity's confusion was all over her face as she lifted from the floor and headed down the stairs. She opened the front door irritated at the intrusion.

How dumb does he think I am?

Upon hearing the door swing open he spun from looking to the street, flowers in hand.

"These are for you. I think we got off on the wrong foot."

"What are you doing here?" She asked without taking the flowers from his extended hand.

"I really need a tutor. I'd be willing to pay you."

"I'm not interested."

"Please, here," he extended the flowers even further.

"Thank you," she said as she finally took the flowers from his hand.

"I know you don't know me and you're new here. But, I think you must have the wrong impression of me."

"What makes you think that? Just because I'm saying no to you and you're not used to that?"

"Well, that's part of it," he admitted with a chuckle then continued.

"I kinda like that. I really do need your help and not a starry-eyed girl trying to impress me."

"What do you want from me? You need someone to do your homework so you can stay on the team?"

"NO! I need to be tutored in math."

"Let me guess you need a passing grade to get your football scholarship or something."

"Something like that, I need an excellent grade to ensure I get the academic scholarship I'm competing for."

17

"Oh!" Serenity stood with a little embarrassment on her face.

"You didn't strike me as the judgmental type but you clearly have your mind made up about me."

Serenity's stature softened some. He was right. She was being overly defensive for what appeared no reason. It wasn't at all like her to be so oppositional.

What has gotten into me?

"You're right, I'm sorry. I'll never make friends that way huh?"

"Maybe one day it'll work for you," Trenton said with a shrug and a grin.

Serenity chuckled.

"Oh, there's a smile. So beautiful," he looked at her differently in that moment.

"When are you available?"

"So, you'll help me?"

"I suppose, I can try."

"Sunday is the only day I can do that wouldn't be too late. We have practice daily."

"Come Sunday around four, we'll see if you're a lost cause or not."

"Thank you."

He was so excited he hugged her; Serenity stood still not returning the embrace because it surprised her and she instantly felt a connection in that embrace. Trenton released her noticing the awkward look on her face.

"I'm sorry. I didn't mean to over step, I just really appreciate it."

"Well, you make it kinda hard to say no, stalking my house and all," Serenity said jokingly.

With that he retreated agreeing to be there Sunday for his session.

After returning to the privacy of her room she exploded in excitement. She couldn't believe he'd hugged her and it felt so genuine. Standing in the full length mirror she could see the glow on her face.

"What was that about?" Her mother asked, appearing behind her in the doorway.

"Nothing, Mother. He wants me to tutor him is all."

"Um hmm, he's a looker, isn't he?"

"You spying on me, I see."

"No such thing,

I just looked out the window for a short time."

"Um hmm," Serenity mumbled with a smirk.

****

Serenity and Trenton started spending a lot of time together. It became more than tutoring; they ate lunch together daily and whatever free time Trenton had. She'd learned more about him as a person. Not only was he excelling on the football field but also academically. He worked part-time at the local hardware store, sang in the church choir and volunteered at the homeless shelter.

As she thought about the night of her prom it dawned on her why she was thinking of him in this moment. The last time she remembered looking at herself in an elegant dress with her hair uncommonly in place was that night. She was positioned now, with her mother behind her, just as she'd done that night. Serenity's prom gown was blue to symbolize Trenton's final college choice of Michigan University. She donned a gold sash to top off the look.

She remembered glancing at her watch thinking Trenton was late. Then she remembered the worry that suddenly hit her. Lydia sat next to Serenity holding her hand in comfort as she sat waiting and worrying with Trenton's now, hour-long tardiness. When the phone rang, it startled Serenity. She dared not answer. It was best her father pick up the call. When Harold knocked on her bedroom door then opened it without awaiting her permission, she held her breath.

"Smooch," was all he said.

Serenity collapsed in tears, she saw the gloom all over his face. Running to her to console his daughter he hugged her tightly as he explained that there had been an accident. Trenton had been killed in route to retrieve his date. What was to be a glorious day for Serenity had turned into a treacherous one.

She shook off the feeling of gloom as she now stood seeing a glimpse of Trenton's charming face smiling in the mirror giving her the thumbs up. That was his approval, not that she needed confirmation but it certainly gave her peace.

Baxter

When he first met Serenity, Baxter knew he wanted her for the rest of his life. More than the yearning to meet her and the rainbow hues that surrounded her, he yearned to be hers. He watched as some colors brightened and dimmed in their first encounter and he knew he could spend an eternity learning her, caring for her, cherishing her, and loving her. He wasn't sure that she knew it yet. But that light that opened up his soul when they touched was all he needed. Baxter knew something and everything was special about Serenity. It was his mission to find out what all that encompassed.

He watched her for a week through the bookstore window, afraid to approach her again. Even though, he knew she was meant for him, he wasn't sure he was ready for her. Baxter wasn't afraid to love; he wasn't afraid of rejection. He was afraid of not being in control. He could tell Serenity would cause him to abandon every protocol he'd adopted. The things he guarded would no longer be inaccessible. Usually, when it came to relationships he knew how to proceed. All he had to do was watch the colors, Serenity's were indecipherable. Then there was his 'ability'. He was afraid of whether she would accept it, could understand it or would she run from it. That was a must for anyone he was to be with for the rest of his life. His apprehension of meeting with her again hinged mostly on that fact.

Baxter had been crushed when Janice began looking at him as if he were a leper. There were very few women Baxter would even bother to get into a serious relationship with. A few, he went further than expected despite some reservations. Janice was one woman he never doubted, felt no ill will, no venom in her bite. They'd dated for months and everything was going wonderfully. He thought she may be the one of his dreams. The aura she owned was multicolored and bright. They had many deep conversations, spent many nights up laughing, playing, movie watching. She was accepting, caring, sensible and open minded (seemingly). The day he told her his secret was forever etched in his mind.

"Jay (his nickname for her) I have to tell you something."

"What is it?"

They'd just finished dinner at his place and were cleaning the kitchen together. Baxter was filled with warmth in his heart and it urged him to tell her before they moved further. He knew he wanted more. Comfort and peace was around them.

"I'm not sure how you'll handle this," he said as he turned to her fully and stopped washing the dish in his hand.

Janice saw the seriousness in his face and gave him her full attention.

"What is it? I'm sure we can work through whatever it is."

"I do hope so. It's something about me you should know."

"Don't tell me you're gay," she said jokingly.

"No, nothing of the sort."

"Whew!" she said with a laugh.

As he looked at her smile and the light blue surrounding her he was sure everything would be ok.

"Well, I figured out some time ago I have a special ability/gift so to speak."

"Which is?" she asked as her blue darkened a bit.

"It's kinda hard to explain but put simply, I can see auras and feel emotions."

"Everyone can feel emotions, what do you mean see auras? I mean I see peoples' faces brighten."

"I don't mean my own emotions. I can sense others' emotions without knowing them or even trying."

He watched her blue hue darken.

"As far as the aura thing, I mean more in depth than that. For example, I can tell you're not very comfortable with this conversation. Though, your facial expression hasn't changed much, your aura went from a light sky blue to nearly a deep purple."

"This sounds demonic to me."

"Demonic? I don't see how you draw that conclusion." Baxter stated, confused.

"What are you an alien or something?"

"I never said anything of such."

"I was just asking if that's what you believed. You sound a bit mental to me."

"Mental? Because you can't understand or because you don't want to?"

"I was never taught to believe any one person could have special powers. Are you some kind of mutant? Is that why you like those sci-fi movies so much, X-men and all that?"

"You know I can't really tell you why or how. But I guess that would be the simplest way to explain."

"You were right. I don't know how to take this."

He could feel her confusion and there was fear and some anger.

"Well, if you want to take some time to talk."

"No. I'd like to think this through on my own," she cut him off.

"Oh, ok."

Janice gathered her things then left without another word. He knew when the door closed he'd seen the last of her. There was a gray cloud that followed her and lingered in the air after she left.

As much as Serenity seemed to be for him, he feared when the day would come to tell her all of this. So, he waited, watched, and studied her through a glass from afar as if admiring a beautiful creature which was being held captive. The day came when he'd built more questions in his mind than he'd had when he first discovered her rainbow. He decided to abandon his obsession. No longer would Baxter sit across from the bookstore wondering what Serenity did for a living, why she seemed to talk to herself more often than anyone else, what she cooked at night or even what she ate. It was beginning to consume him.

His reason for not approaching her was pointless because control had already been lost. He'd gotten up the nerve to just walk in and ask her out on a date. Just as he was crossing the street he watched as a gentleman joined her in her sacred place. He watched as the smile on her face spread and her colors shot to the sky. Serenity was happy to see this man, a young handsome man. In all the time he'd watched her, never had he seen her so happy.

With all the time of his longing, it never dawned on him she would have a suitor.

Why wouldn't she? She's beautiful.

He could kick himself for taking that fact for granted. Where had this guy been all this time? Why hadn't he seen him before? Baxter's heart sunk. It was time to let go of the dream he thought he'd just about caught. Instead of crossing the street he retreated to the restaurant behind him and found a seat at the bar. Drowning his sorrows seemed in order.

Serenity

After her first encounter with Baxter, Serenity ran right in telling Janice all about it.

"I met a guy today. He was beautiful."

"Really, what happened?"

"I was my usual unkempt self, I spilled my tea. He bought me a new one."

"Is that it?"

"Well, yeah sort of. He came and sat with me out the blue."

"Did he ask you out?"

"No."

"Did he ask for your number?"

"No."

"What the hell kinda meeting is that?"

"I don't know. It was something magical about it," Serenity said with a shrug.

"Did you see fireworks or something?" Janice asked sarcastically.

"Actually, I kinda did. When I touched his hand, I saw this bright light, briefly......... I think."

"You think? Either you did or you didn't."

"I saw something but then when we shook hands, it didn't happen again. You know I second guess myself."

"You confuse yourself more than necessary. Life is already confusing," Janice stated in annoyance.

"Tell me about it. You know you're no help for encouraging a girl."

"I keep it real. What are you gonna do if you see him again?"

"Nothing, I doubt I will say a word."

"Oh, you're gonna do something. You're gonna ask him out if he doesn't ask you. If it was as magical as you say. You'll see him again."

"There is NO way I'll ask him out."

"Yes, you will. I feel it. You were excited at a touch."

"You didn't feel anything. You're just tryna get me to make a fool of myself. If he wanted me, he would've asked."

"I wouldn't want to see you embarrassed, no matter how much you get on my nerves. I'm serious. I don't want you to do what I did and let a great man go because of fear. What's his name?"

"Uhhh, I forgot."

"How the hell you forget the man of your dreams?"

"I didn't say all that. I just meant it was something different about him. Brian was his name."

"Ok, we are going to come up with a game plan for Brian. When you see him again, you'll be prepared."

It turned out that Janice was right and Serenity was prepared. She thought it was ridiculous at the time but, they rehearsed what she would do. This particular day she'd left the bookstore to venture over to the restaurant across the street. She was elated. Christian had come to see her. She hadn't seen him since graduating college. Though they kept in touch, it had been many years since she laid eyes on him.

Christian was the second great love of her life. The very first day of college he went out of his way to make her interact with him. Even when she attempted those one-word answers to his questions, he demanded more.

"It's like pulling teeth to get you to talk. You do have teeth, don't you?" He asked, which made her laugh and show them all.

From that day forth they were pretty inseparable. Christian protected her from anyone he felt she needed protection from. The playboys stayed away, the envious women were shut down. In return, Serenity protected him in her own way. Junior year, they moved in together against the wishes of her father. But, she was a grown woman and he'd grown accustom to Chris. He just didn't believe it was proper for them to 'shack up'.

They'd had their disagreements over the years but there was no bond like the one they shared. Graduation day was both joyous and tearful. Christian had gotten a job in New York and was off to his life while Serenity was staying in Michigan to pursue her career. But there he was in front of her and she didn't want to let him go so fast. She'd missed him, his antics and his reverence.

So, there they were going over to grab a bite to eat laughing about Christian's insistence that Serenity have a drink with him. Serenity looks up and there sits Baxter (or Brian as she thought of him at the time). Already in an awesome mood and full of courage, prepared for this chance meeting; she strolled right up to Brian (Baxter). It seemed; he looked her way as soon as she walked in as if he felt her come through the door. The look on his face was of surprise and glee.

"We meet again," Serenity said.

"Yes, this time you walked into my world."

"I suppose I did."

"I didn't think you ever left the bookstore."

Baxter cursed himself for saying that. He was already a few drinks into drowning his sorrows and realized he'd said a bit too much.

"What do you mean? Have you been watching me?" Serenity looked at him inquisitively.

"Oh no, nothing like that. I drive by a few times a week and it seems you're always in the window." *Good save.*

Serenity looked at him with scrutiny.

"Um hmm, well how about we stop running into each other and just exchange numbers?"

Just when Baxter was about to answer, Christian clears his throat. The air in Baxter's balloon expanded and exploded. He'd almost forgotten about him.

"Oh, how rude, this is my best friend Christian."

"How are you Christian?" Baxter said as he extended his hand.

"Chile, I'm great and you are fine!" Christian said as he extended his hand.

"Maybe you can help me convince Miss Thing to take a drink."

"He knows good and well I don't drink."

"Well, I don't think just one little drink would hurt. We can get you something light, maybe a Fuzzy Navel."

"Uh, no! She can have that, but she's taking a shot with me. I haven't seen her in ten months of Sundays and we gotta relive our college days," Christian said.

"I'll let you fight that battle, I'm not in, yet. I don't wanna mess up my chances," Baxter said and gave Serenity a sultry look which made her blush.

"You're a smart man," Serenity said.

"Listen, I'll let you two catch up. Give me a call sometime. If not, I know where to find you," Baxter said as he scribbled his number on a napkin and gave it to her.

"Nice seeing you again," Serenity said.

"It was good meeting you, sexy man," Christian said as they headed to a table for a seat.

In college, Christian had always been the social one, popular and noticed, while Serenity tagged along. But they'd shared secrets without judgement. Serenity accepted Chris as he was at a time in his life when he thought he could no longer bear the weight of his sorrows. He felt alone in a world he thought he was meant to own. Just before leaving for college Christian came out of the proverbial closet to his parents. Things got ugly, so ugly in fact he hasn't spoken to his parents since. They never showed up to fashion shows he'd invited them to nor his graduation. Though he tried to hide it, Serenity knew it still hurt. And no matter where or how deep he'd buried that pain it was still there. So, when he showed up insisting on drinks she knew he just needed to talk. And that they did, into the wee hours of the night.

Baxter

For Baxter, being all wrong about Serenity's male friend was like hitting the lottery. When he left the bar the grin on his face was visible from miles away. His brain's gears began to turn. He couldn't wait until the next day to pop up on her at the bookstore to ask her out. There was no way holding his breath waiting for her to call was an option. Baxter was determined to solidify his spot in her life as soon as possible. He was scared straight. When he approached Serenity, she was not at all surprised by his appearance nor did she give any opposition at his request for a date. The biggest worry that plagued his mind was where to take her, it had to be special.

Baxter was pleasantly surprised when he received a text from Serenity a few days before their date. At first, he feared she was going to cancel on him. But, she just wanted to make small talk and get the basics out of the way before their date. Though, he was more inclined to telephone calls, he was comfortable with texting her. His nervousness would have come across over the phone. However, through text messages he could appear clever, cool, calm and together. Some of the things that plagued his mind had been put to rest. She was a freelance writer, book reviewer and sometimes substitute taught.

For their first date, Baxter wanted to do more than take her to dinner or a movie. He wanted to make a lasting impression. By the time the brainstorming was done the list was formulated for all future awesome dates. First, he had to decipher what Serenity's adventurous limits were. Deciding on a nice hot air balloon ride and picnic, he headed to the store. Recalling that she didn't drink he purchased sparkling cider, fruit, cheese and crackers.

The morning of, he'd carefully packed a basket including a cold pack to keep everything chilled. Heading out to meet her several minutes before he was scheduled to, his anxiousness began to get the best of him. It seemed as if he had a choke hold on the steering wheel, he gripped it so tightly. Baxter gave himself a pep talk, ensuring his breathing slowed and his pulse became steady. He had insisted on picking Serenity up like a proper gentleman but she refused. She agreed to meet in the parking lot of the nearest mall.

Serenity arrived about five minutes after Baxter.

She was early.

His phone rang.

"Hello," Baxter said.

"Hi, I'm here over by the Italian Restaurant."

It took a second for Baxter to answer, his words caught in his throat. Her voice was so melodic. It was the first time he'd heard it through the phone.

"I'm here, I'll drive around to meet you. What are you in?"

Serenity let him know what vehicle to look for and they disconnected. Within two minutes Baxter pulled his car in the space beside hers. He exited his vehicle as did she. The chuckle from deep within couldn't be helped when the realization of what Serenity was doing came forth. Her phone was out and the flash was going off. She'd taken a picture of his license plate with him included.

"Don't laugh. I want you to see this. So you know if I come up missing they'll know who to question," Serenity said as she pressed a button on her phone then retired it to her small purse.

"Trust me, if you're missing it will be because you want to be."

"Is that so?"

"It is."

She gave him a sideways look then mumbled something under her breath which he didn't catch.

"So, are you ready to get this show on the road?"

"As ready as I can be," she responded.

"Well, let's get going we have a little ride ahead of us," Baxter said as he led her to the passenger side of his vehicle and opened it for her.

Once in the car, buckled up and ready to go he looked into her eyes.

"You look very beautiful."

"Thank you."

He could tell she was humbled not only by the way she averted eye contact or the blush that now flushed her cheeks. The pink hue that enveloped her brightened and nearly took over. Pleased with himself, the car went from park to drive and they were on their way. During the nearly hour ride they kept the conversation light, on music, art, hobbies and etc. Steadily, Baxter stole glances of her. Even though she was dressed casually, the way her clothes draped her body made the ensemble appear elegant, in his eyes anyway.

"How do you know I'm not afraid of heights?" Serenity asked when they pulled into the location.

A look of terror spread across Baxter's face, he looked at her and she looked back stone faced. Serenity erupted in laughter.

"You're safe, I'm not afraid."

It was visible that Baxter finally released a breath he was holding by the upheaval of his shoulders.

"I see you're a jokester."

"Not really, I'm more, full of sarcasm than anything else."

The date couldn't have gone any better than he'd planned it. Baxter was pleased with the outcome and Serenity's company. She was impressed that he'd remembered she wasn't a drinker and the cheese and fruit selections. He could tell by the twinkle in her eyes. As the day neared its end, Baxter began to dread having to leave her. After arriving back at her vehicle, he again, opened her car door.

"I really had a great time," Serenity said as she exited the car.

"That is mutual, my angel."

"I'll make sure to let you know when I get home."

"Please do, I'll be waiting."

Baxter wasn't sure if it was safe to embrace her, though he really wanted to kiss her. She was the first to make a gesture for a hug. That relieved him. He wasn't alone in the thought.

Just as they were about to release the embrace, Baxter turned his head to give her a light peck on the cheek. So happens, Serenity was in the same motion and their lips met. Baxter squinted.

"What was that?" Serenity asked.

"I'm sorry, I was trying to kiss your cheek."

"Not that. You didn't see that?"

"See what?"

"Nothing"

"What did you see?"

"It was nothing it must have been a car or something."

"Get home safe," Baxter said as he made sure she was seated in her car.

"I will," she responded as he closed her door.

More than ever, Baxter was sure that Serenity was meant for him. Everything about their date was wonderful from his point of view. The more he was with her, the more he loved all the things about her. She was unpredictable, it was refreshing for him. Even though how she felt was written all around her, it was in a language he had yet to learn. He was now desperate to learn her language, her body, her thoughts, her mind, heart and even her soul.

Serenity

"Well, how was it?" Janice asked as Serenity laid across her bed in a daze.

She'd walked in the house as if she were floating. Stars in her eyes, music playing in her ears, nothing could ruin her week after such a lovely day.

"It was everything and more," Serenity replied.

"What did you do?"

"He took me high in the sky then brought me back to earth and fed me."

"What? English girl, I am not in the mood for your riddles."

"We went in a hot air balloon then had a small picnic."

"That sounds simple and awesome."

"It was awesome," Serenity stated.

"He must be great. You sound like you're singing."

"We kissed."

"You did what?! Not you."

"It wasn't like a kiss, kiss. It was an accidental kiss."

"How do you kiss by accident?"

"Because, never mind all that. I saw the light again. It flashed when our lips touched. I think he saw it too. As a matter of fact, I know he did. He squinted as if shielding his eyes."

41

"Really?!"

"Absolutely."

"When are you going to see him again?"

"I don't know. We didn't say. I'm supposed to let him know I made it home. I'm going to call right now and invite him over for dinner one-day next week."

"You are going to invite him here?"

"Yes!"

"Wow. That kiss must have been magical."

"Completely, I think he's the one."

Janice didn't say another word. Serenity retrieved her phone and made the phone call.

****

Serenity spent all day in preparation for this meal. Moreover, the visit, she had never invited any other man into her home. It took her all day to decide what to wear. Janice thought it was ludicrous that Serenity put so much fuss into what to wear in her own home. Finally, deciding on her garbs she then couldn't make a decision on the menu. She didn't want to do anything too extraordinary but not too simple. Serenity even mulled over what music she would have playing the entire night. She put a playlist together and had everything all set when Baxter arrived.

When Baxter arrived, Serenity opened the front door and left it ajar for him. He knocked and she yelled for him to come on in.

"I'll be right out," she said from parts unknown to Baxter.

"Ok."

"Go ahead, have a seat I'm getting the chicken from the oven."

Serenity removed the parmesan crusted chicken from the oven and sat it on the top to cool a bit. When she rounded the corner from the kitchen Baxter was seated on the couch and jumped up at the sight of her.

"You don't have to get up."

"Sure, I do. I must hug and greet my hostess."

They hugged then Serenity motioned for him to return to his seat.

"Make yourself comfortable. Everything is pretty much ready. I'm just waiting for the crescent rolls to brown."

"No rush. How was your day?"

"Uneventful and yours?"

"About the same."

"Well, we can eat when you want I have salad to start."

"There's no time like the present."

"Go ahead have a seat at the dining room table."

"First, I'd like to wash my hands, and then I'd like to help you set the table."

"The rest room is right there," she said pointing to the small half bath near the front door.

"Don't worry, I got the table."

By the time Baxter came out everything was on display in the center of her small dining table.

"It looks great," he said.

"Thanks, it's been a while since I've cooked for anyone else. I have cereal on standby just in case."

Baxter chuckled as they sat.

"Well, dig in."

She prepared his plate getting some of everything in front of him. Baxter waited until Serenity fixed her plate.

"Would you like something to drink?"

"Water is fine."

Serenity got up to get him a glass of water, once returning to the table she noticed he hadn't touched his food.

"Don't tell me I need to pull out the cereal? You haven't touched your food."

"I was simply waiting for you. I can't eat before you."

Serenity was honored, proud, humbled and impressed all in one. And in Baxter's eyes, it had shown in her bright gold hue. When Baxter took his first bite, Serenity watched for his reaction. He seemed please but, the sure indication was his request for more.

"I've never seen you with your hair up. Your face is absolutely gorgeous."

"Thank you," Serenity said as she blushed and lowered her eyes.

"Why do you do that?"

"What?"

"Look away when I compliment you, are you ashamed?"

"No, it's not that. I just think I am ordinary," Serenity said with a shrug.

"I think you're far from ordinary," he said as he lifted her chin with his index finger and thumb.

They were now peering at each other eye to eye.

"I guess beauty is in the eye of the beholder."

Where is Janice?" She thought.

"This beholder thinks you are the most beautiful creature on earth," Baxter declared.

"Would you like coffee, dessert or drink? I remember what you drink I think. Was it Hennessey?"

"Yes, that's correct but no thank you. I'm stuffed and I don't think I can be responsible for my actions if I were to drink."

"What actions might those be?"

"We'll never know."

They laughed together. After chatting for a few minutes, Serenity suggested they move to the living room to be more comfortable. She offered to turn on a movie but Baxter wanted to talk. It didn't bother her at all; she wanted to know more about him. She wanted to know everything, in fact. It was her turn to ask the questions. She felt more comfortable on her own turf. Serenity found out about his family, sibling, parents, childhood. She asked him about his past relationships, had his heart been broken. And he told her the story about Jay, a girl that left him high and dry when he thought she accepted him completely.

"Are you scared to love again?" Serenity asked.

"I was for a long while but not anymore," he said as he looked directly into her eyes.

"You plan on getting married one day?"

"That's the goal. I'm kinda thinking, I'm going to marry you."

"Get outta here."

"I'm serious."

"You're crazy. Should I be calling the police now?"

"Do what you like but, you mark my words."

Serenity looked at him with one eyebrow raised, searching his face to see if he was serious.

If only he knew what baggage I came with.

Baxter looked at his watch.

"I don't want to keep you too late. I better get home. I have an early morning anyway."

"I enjoyed your company," Serenity said.

"And I yours, until next time lovely lady," Baxter said as he stood and extended his arms for a hug.

This time, they embraced and there was no mistake when they kissed. It was purposeful. Serenity closed her eyes so that the fireworks wouldn't startle her this time. She peeked mid-kiss. It was as if the sky opened up and the sun was shining down on them right there in the middle of her living room at midnight. Pulling away from him because she didn't know what to make of it, she chuckled.

"That was something else," she said.

"Yes. It was. And I better go."

She walked him to the door and watched as he made his way down the stairs. Janice came up behind her.

"Is that him? I tried to stay out your way. I didn't get to see his face."

"Hey!" Serenity called to Baxter.

He spun around in response to her.

"Make sure to call me when you make it home."

"I will," he answered before entering his car and pulling off.

Serenity closed the door and turned to Janice.

"Satisfied?"

Janice looked as if she had suddenly become ill.

"What's wrong?" Serenity asked.

"That's him? His name isn't Brian, it's Baxter."

"Yeah, I forgot to tell you that. Umm, how do you know that?"

"Because Serenity that's **him**."

Baxter

"I'm getting married," Baxter said into the phone.

"To who?" Clay asked.

"Her name is Serenity and she is the most beautiful creature on earth."

"When?"

"I don't know."

"Oooook? How long have you been with her?"

"I'm not."

"What the fuck are you talking about, dude? How you getting married to someone you don't even know?"

"I know her, I met her, and I can see through her, I'm telling you she's the one."

"Does she know this?"

"Maybe. I told her but, I don't think she believed me."

"You sound crazy, slow down. Give me the run down."

Baxter began to tell his brother about the chronicle of Serenity. The minute he'd left Serenity's home he began making plans in his head. One thing he was sure of was that he wasn't letting that woman get away from him. The sky had opened up and shown him the light. Baxter dictated to Clayton the series of events at what seemed a mile a minute.

"Well, I see you're excited about this one," Clayton said with a hint of sarcasm.

"She's it! Serenity is what I've been waiting for all my life. She's beyond beautiful, intelligent, witty, and adventurous."

"Slow your roll man. Do you even know her last name?"

"It will be White in no time soon. That's all I need to know."

"You're not usually one to throw caution to the wind. Did she put it on you?" Clayton chuckled.

"We haven't slept together, if that's what you're asking. I'm not you Clay, that's not the first thing on my mind."

"You don't have to be like me to get pu—have sex."

"I don't lead my life with the head between my legs. She's my soul mate, I guarantee it. Everything I thought I'd ever want in a woman, she's got it."

"You know I'm not going to discourage you. I'd just like to point out that you don't know what she has that you weren't looking for, yet. But I trust you know what you're doing."

"Thank you. Just be happy for me."

"I am but I can't just turn off my skepticism."

"You'll see, write this down. I told you this day she would be my wife. May not be tomorrow but, she will be."

"Well, since you put the cart before the horse already. When do I get to meet her?"

"I'll let you know. Trust me it will be soon."

"This will be interesting."

They chatted a while longer then disconnected. Baxter found it hard to fall asleep. Once he did, his slumber was blissful.

Sometime midafternoon, Baxter glanced down at his phone knowing he couldn't have possibly missed a call but wishing that maybe he had. He expected a ring from Serenity that had yet to come. Anxious and now unsure of himself he'd picked up his phone to call then put it down several times. The assuredness he toted late into the night and early this morning was beginning to fade. His (what he thought) well laid plans were already faltering. Before even getting out of bed this morning Baxter pulled out his tablet and ordered Serenity a fresh bouquet of lovely flowers. He knew they HAD to have been delivered by now. That should have led way for Serenity to be the one to call first, just to say thank you, at least.

He'd put extra thought into what kind of flower, what color and changed his mind a zillion times. He settled on every color tulip they had.

A rainbow to represent her rainbow.

The day ticked by and his anticipation grew. When Serenity finally did call, the ring didn't even complete its cycle before the phone was to his ear.

"Hello, how are you?"

"I'm good. How are you?" Serenity replied.

"Not bad."

"I loved the flowers, thank you. You should've told me. I've been out all day."

"Well, a surprise isn't a surprise if I tell you about it."

"I suppose not. It was a pleasant one."

"I'm glad you liked," Baxter reveled.

"They are wonderfully colorful."

"That just seemed like you."

"Very much so," Serenity acknowledged

There was a silent lull for a few seconds.

"Listen, I had a really great time with you. I'd like to see you again, soon. Can we do dinner?" Baxter confessed.

"Yes, we can. When did you have in mind?"

"Tonight!" Baxter said louder than he'd expected.

"That's short notice but I can manage that I suppose."

"I didn't mean to be presumptuous, if you don't have no other plans, of course."

"I don't. It's fine. Your company is welcomed."

"I'm glad to hear that. So, is eight o'clock fine with you?"

"Yes."

"I'd like to pick you up properly, if you don't mind."

"Seeing as how you already know where I live. That would be acceptable."

"Good, I'll see you at eight."

"And how shall I dress, casual dining or fancy dinner?"

"Fancy dinner but not formal"

"Ok…."

"Don't change your mind on me now."

"I'm not. Just thinking of what to wear."

"Good, I'm looking forward to seeing your choice."

"I'll be ready," she said with a smile.

"See you then."

After disconnecting, Baxter nearly did a cartwheel. He gained his confidence back in that instant. His focus back to winning her, heart and soul, he made reservations for dinner.

Serenity

Serenity felt like she was floating. It had been three months since she'd started going out with Baxter. There had only been a few days that they hadn't seen one another. And she found herself missing him those days when he wasn't around. But she knew he hadn't completely committed to trusting her. Serenity knew he was holding something back. Over the course of the last few months, they'd been spending time getting to know all the ends and outs of one another's lives. There were plenty things they'd shared and Serenity was ready for him to let go of what he'd been holding back. She'd decided in order to move forward (which she hoped he wanted) she had to force his hand. He needed to tell her his everything and she was ready to show him that she was willing to do the same.

"I want you here about nine. He's coming over at seven, which gives us time to eat and then ease into talking."

"Are you sure about this? You don't have to do this for me."

"Janice, you are the one who told me to be completely honest. This is it, all or nothing. I can't keep going on this path knowing he's hiding parts of himself. And that I'm keeping secrets from him."

"I'm nervous," Janice said.

"YOU?! How do you think I feel? Hell, I might drink some wine."

"Nine o'clock, it is. As long as you're sure."

"I'm sure. I want this."

Just as planned, after dinner Serenity and Baxter were seated on the couch having a light discussion. He must have seen the expression on her change.

"Are you ok?"

"Yes, there's something I need to talk to you about."

"What is it? You know you can tell me anything," Baxter said as he moved closer with a look of concern on his face.

"You know, I believe that. But do you think you can tell me anything?"

"Of course, I do."

"I'm not so sure. I feel like you are holding something back from me."

"I'm not sure what you're talking about."

"Ok, let me ask you something then."

"Anything," he said sincerely.

"What happened between you and Janice?"

Baxter's eyes popped out a bit then she could tell he was trying to keep his facial expression stoic.

"We talked about that. She just left. Why are you concerned about her? That was years ago."

"She has something to do with what you're holding back."

"How could you know that?"

Serenity took a deep breath before she began to speak.

"I've never done this before; it scares me to death. But, I want you to know I'm committed to being with you and continuing to grow together."

"I couldn't imagine being without you, already."

"Let me get through this before you say anything."

"Ok, I'll just listen."

"We've become really close over the past months. I want everything with you. You've been holding something back and I know it. There is no better way to show you that you can trust me with your secrets than to show you all of me as well."

She paused, took another deep breath.

"You know we've talked about how I don't socialize much, how I keep to myself. I'm so used to giving some generic explanation for that. I've always been a loner, the odd one out, black sheep or whatever other name for outcasts people come up with. I want you to accept me."

"I do honey," Baxter interrupted.

Serenity gave him a look and he held his hands up as if surrendering, remembering he's supposed to just let her speak.

"Baxter, I really think I'm falling, **have** fallen in love with you and before I can really give into the feeling of 'us' it must be full disclosure."

Baxter's mouth dropped with her words and he was so ready to tell her he loved her too but he held his tongue awaiting her punch line.

"This is so hard to say," Serenity proclaimed as she put her face in her hands.

"Just tell me," he said as he placed his hand to her knee.

Serenity removed her hands from her face, avoiding his eyes. She began to explain.

"I know Janice; she's been my friend for years. When we first met I had no idea who you were. And I feel as if I should have told you after our second date but she didn't want me to lose you too."

"How do you know Janice? What did she tell you about us?"

"She used to live here and she told me everything."

"Everything?"

"Yes, but there's something she wanted to tell you and she's coming to tell you. Will you be open to listen?"

"This is strange, are you trying to play some sort of game with me?" Baxter asked as he tried to move away from her on the couch.

"Please don't do that, don't shy away from me."

"Serenity, I don't know who the woman you've been friends with is or what game she's playing but it's not the Janice I thought I once loved."

"Yes, but it is Baxter. She saw you as you were leaving the first time you were here. She'd told me all about how she ran away from you. We spent hours talking about how she regretted losing you and not giving you a reason for her actions. All before I'd even met you."

"Serenity, believe me this woman is an imposter and we'll see when she gets here."

"Janice will be here in a moment."

"Not the Janice I once knew."

"YES! Baxter, **hear** what I'm saying to you. Janice told me all about your gift. For months, I've watched your eyes twinkle and face change with my every feeling wondering which color I wore for you."

Baxter looked at Serenity in disbelief. His mouth hung ajar and head slightly titled. He couldn't fathom what he was hearing.

"How do you know this? No one knows about that but Clayton."

"And you told Janice," Serenity said in a soft tone.

"Janice didn't understand it; she didn't want to."

"She understood it. What you didn't understand is that she wasn't running from you. Janice was afraid of her own guilt."

"Guilt?" He asked full of confusion.

"Janice never told you that her mother had been in a mental hospital for most of her life. She never explained to you that for years she thought her mother was insane proclaiming to hear voices and see figures."

"That had nothing to do with me."

"No. But when you revealed your gift at first, she felt trapped in a world of crazy. Like you were the best thing that happened to her and you were crazy too. She couldn't deal with the thought of dealing with that as she had with her mother. It ate at her that maybe she'd been wrong about you the entire time. Then, her thoughts turned to the fact that maybe you weren't crazy. Which would mean maybe her mother wasn't either. She agonized over that, thinking her mother had been treated unfairly. She wanted to come back to you. Then she thought it best to let you heal and move on."

"I can't believe what you're telling me. How do you know all this?" Baxter inquired.

"I told you Janice and I have been friends for years, she told me so much about the love of her life. When she gets here you can ask all the questions you want. Anything you need to validate her identity."

"It's not possible.

A breeze blew through the house, a magazine paper rustled on the table and the candle light flickered.

"But it is. She's here."

"Serenity," Baxter said as he grabbed her hand looking into her eyes.

"Yes," she said returning his gaze.

"Janice is dead."

"I know."

Baxter

At first, Baxter didn't know whether to be ecstatic or fearful when Serenity talked to him. When she first began talking, he thought maybe she was going to say she was seeing someone else or she had some illegitimate child she gave up for adoption as a teenager. Never could he imagine what actually came from her lips. He couldn't deny that he was relieved. There was no more worry if she could accept him completely. She'd, unbeknownst to him, had the same worry in regards to him. Though he still had many questions and was willing to accept it all, the shock still hadn't worn off weeks later.

The night he 'talked' to Janice would forever be etched in his mind. Not only because he'd gotten much needed closure but because it had also solidified his love for Serenity. He gained so much more insight as to how he'd felt about her. It was clear in his mind. Now, more than ever that they belonged together. That night opened his soul for her to take and she in turn was giving him hers. When Serenity said Janice was there he looked around several times.

"Where is she?"

"Janice is standing next to you," Serenity said.

He unconsciously turned as if he would see her.

"Tell me you're joking," he said to Serenity.

"I'm not. You have a gift. So do I. I see, hear and can even feel spirits. It took me a long time to control it and even differentiate them from others. I promise the day you introduced yourself to me, I had to question if you were even real."

61

"This is...... I don't know what to say this is," Baxter stated.

"It's crazy, weird, crazy, ridiculous; it's all of that."

"Unbelievable."

"That too," Serenity said.

"I want to tell Janice I'm sorry for putting all that on her when she wasn't ready."

"She says you shouldn't feel any guilt about her death. It wasn't because of you. She had other things to resolve."

"I want to thank her for the time I spent with her."

"She wants to thank you. She says you were put into her life to help her open up her mind to possibilities so that she could have a life with the mother she never had."

"Wow, I've thought so many times of what I would say to her if I ever saw her again. Now, I can't think much of any of that."

"I don't think there is much to say. I won't be mad if you want to tell her you love her. I know she will always have a place in your heart. She was the first woman you ever felt you could open up to. That takes a lot."

"She will always be in my heart. I'm not angry with her."

"She's smiling and says she loves you also. She says nothing was ever able to replace to hole in her heart you were ripped from."

Then Serenity smiled, nodded and said she loved Janice too. Baxter wasn't sure what was going on but he knew they were having their own conversation. That breeze from before returned, he watched the candle light waver again.

"Is she gone?" Baxter asked.

"Yes, she won't be back. She told me she loved me and that her time with you was past. It's now my time," Serenity said as she touched Baxter's cheek.

There was an orange glow from her hand to his face, he didn't have to pretend not to see. He leaned into her hand then leaned over to embrace her. They sat silently listening to their synchronized breaths allowing every feeling to flow between them. When Baxter pulled away, he noticed the tears Serenity tried to will to stay in her eyes.

"What's wrong?"

"Nothing, this is SO overwhelming and beautiful all at once."

"I have so many questions," Baxter replied.

"So do I."

"You first."

"So, that first day at the book store, did you see that damn light when you touched me?"

"Yes," Baxter chuckled.

"Making me think I'm damn crazy! You didn't flinch."

"I'm used to it. I learned how not to react when it happens or when I see things."

"So, the sky did open up and shine down on us when we kissed the first time?" Serenity said with excitement.

"Yes, baby. It did!"

"Oh, my Gawd! What the hell do you think is going to happen when we have sex?"

"That, I have no idea about," Baxter said as he laughed.

He felt so jovial at the way she was taking it all in and seemed to love every minute of it. They sat nearly the entire night into the early morning barraging one another with questions. They each answered without hesitation. He learned, like him, only her family knew of her gift. She once saw it as a burden, while he always found his helpful.

He was thankful to have the time to reflect on he and Janice's relationship and most importantly that she understood. Janice had found her peace in the bottom of a prescription bottle after her mother did something of the same in an institution. Baxter knew of none of this. He had only found out about her departure through a Google search on one of his reminiscent days. Getting answers made him better and them better together.

As he sat now and thought of it, they absorbed each other that night. They knew it was meant for them to do something great together and they couldn't wait to find out what that was. They were far beyond love, it was destined. He wanted to tell Clayton all about what they shared. But he knew Clay was still apprehensive about talking about those kinds of things. So, he kept it to himself.

****

Baxter had a special weekend planned for Serenity. He called in a lot of favors to achieve his desired atmosphere. As any other time, she was completely oblivious to what was going on. She always made a big deal out of being in the dark but he knew she loved it. Baxter loved to watch her survey the surroundings as the gears in her head churned. The best part was watching her color change every time she made a new discovery or clue to where they were going. When they pulled into a private airfield she turned bright yellow.

"Baxter what in the hell are you up to?" She asked with a smile on her face.

"We've done everything there is to be done in this area. It's time to find somewhere else to date."

"Where are you taking me?"

"Why do you ask me questions?"

"I don't know. Maybe, because I want to know."

"Just come on," Baxter told her.

They approached the small office, Baxter told Serenity to stay outside so she wouldn't hear anything prematurely. When he exited the office, she followed him toward the hangers. They approached a small jet and began boarding.

"How'd you pull this off Mr. Big Shot?" Serenity asked.

"I know people that know Big Shots. It's not me," they laughed.

Two other passengers boarded and they all said their salutations.

"So, where are you guys going?" Serenity asked.

"Same place you are," the woman said.

Serenity looked at her a little put off by her response then looked at Baxter. He began laughing.

"I already told them not to tell you," he said while laughing.

"I'm Jason, this is Tamara," the man said.

"You can call me Tammy," said the woman as she extended her hand to shake with Serenity.

"So, it appears you two know more about what's going on here than I do."

"Does it help if I say you'll love it?" Tammy asked.

"Not really, I knew that already."

They all laughed.

The pilot let everyone know they'd be taking off shortly. Just as they'd closed the door to the plane a panicked look swept Serenity's face.

"We can't take off," Serenity said.

"Relax honey, we'll be fine," Tammy said.

"No, they missed something. We can't take off, yet."

As the plane began to taxi Serenity nearly exploded.

"STOP THE PLANE!"

"Honey, it's ok," Baxter said.

She turned to look at him square in his eyes.

"NO! BAX-TER it's NOT ok!" She said with bucked eyebrows.

Baxter immediately stood and started to the cockpit. It took quite a bit of convincing but he got the pilot to stop. He exited the plane then convinced the ground crew to do their final checks one last time.

Jason and Tammy were visibly annoyed at the delay.

"Apologies, better safe than sorry. If she wants one more assurance to be comfortable, it's better to take this thirty-minute delay than the long ride in the air with her on edge," Baxter explained as he stuck his head back in.

"I understand," Jason said.

"Really, I hope I'm not making you late for anything. Sometimes, I do get a bit ridiculous."

"Honey, thirty minutes ain't gone kill me but something wrong with a plane could. I'll just keep drinking, that makes everything better," Tammy said.

Nearly, an hour later Baxter re-entered the plane, took his seat as they reclosed the doors.

"We're all set and ready for take-off. Everything checks out baby. I watched them check myself," Baxter said as he touched Serenity's hand.

She looked in his eyes and knew that everything was fine. He watched the hunter green color that surrounded her turn lighter then back to an orangey yellow. Serenity glanced out the window every so often to try to decipher where in the world she may be. When her eyes spied crystal blue waters Baxter watched her turn bright yellow again. He knew how much she loved the tropics.

"I'll give you a clue," Baxter said into her ear.

"What's the clue, honey?" She looked at him lovingly.

"We're going somewhere warm."

"Duh! I figured that out."

"Ok, another clue. Somewhere near the water."

This time she didn't say a word she just looked at him blankly.

"Somewhere you always wanted to go. Is that good enough?"

"That's better but that could be a million places," she said as she lightly swatted his arm.

Tammy, who'd been napping alongside Jason, looked up and began to speak.

"I see so much love between you two. You will be together for two lifetimes."

"That's nice of you to say," Baxter said.

"Let her finish," Serenity said cutting him off.

"No matter what life throws at you, remember what I'm telling you. Your love can not be broken. Your bond is to the core. You hear what I say."

"Yes ma'am," Serenity said.

Then Tammy was out again.

"That was strange. She has had a few drinks though," Baxter noted.

"It wasn't Tammy talking. That's why I don't drink," Serenity said then turned her attention back toward the water below as if it were no big deal.

Baxter on the other hand felt like he needed a drink after that. Baxter was full of questions but he thought it best to ask them later away from strange ears.

Serenity

When they arrived in Tahiti, Serenity had no idea what Baxter had in store nor did she care. As she felt the warm air across her face, she thought about how much in love with this man she was. She would never give him up. She didn't dare ask any questions as Baxter led her to an awaiting taxi. He wouldn't have told her anyway. They ended up in a small hut on stilts that hovered over the ocean. Serenity loved the glass floor. She stood watching the wild life beneath her feet for at least ten minutes.

"Baby, this is so wonderful, thank you, thank you, thank you," Serenity said as she wrapped her arms around Baxter.

"No thanks needed. I can't wait to see you in a bathing suit."

"Hush! What are we going to do first?"

"Whatever you want, there are plenty of activities. I figured we'd wait for tomorrow to do all the water sports when we're well rested."

"That's a great idea. I would just love to lay with you in the sand."

"Let's get to it then."

Serenity and Baxter spent the remainder of the day walking the beach, doing light some shopping. They fell asleep in each other's arms listening to the waves. As they stared up at the stars Baxter asked,

"Hey, what was the problem at take off?"

"I'm not sure. But someone appeared and said we couldn't take off yet."

"They didn't find anything wrong with the plane."

"There may not have been. Maybe there was something going on with the pilot or other plane in our path."

"I never thought of that. All I knew is that you had this muted color somewhere between gray and brown. It was strange, something I'd never seen before."

"Sometimes, I don't get clear cut answers. I just know there are reasons."

"And Tammy? Who was that?"

"Are you sure you want to know?"

"I'm sure."

"That was your mother's mother, I believe. She didn't tell me her name; I could just feel her."

Baxter sat there quietly gazing at the stars imagining his family looking down on them.

The next day was packed full with snorkeling, jet skiing and parasailing. Serenity didn't think her life could get any better. As they were preparing to go to dinner, she looked over at him and for a split second she thought she could see a red cloud surrounding him. After a few blinks of the eye it was gone.

They sat in the dining area of the resort, which was a short stroll from their hut. After ordering, Serenity gazed into Baxter eyes.

"You know I love you, don't you?" Serenity asked.

"Yes, I do. It's written all over your face," he sang out.

"Can you ever turn that off?"

"I can block it out sometimes."

"What if I wanted to tell you a lie?"

"You have no reason to."

"That's not the point."

"I don't know what to tell you. I don't even think I could block it out with you. You're so vibrant. I think it would still shine through."

"I love that you can see through me. I guess because I've always wanted people to not see me or see right past me for so long. Showing you everything is like euphoria."

"Like getting high?" he asked with a smile.

"I guess so. I can't get enough of you. I wouldn't care if we were in the backyard, park or across the ocean. I always want to know you can see my heart, mind and soul."

"Those sound like wedding vows."

"Was kinda poetic, huh?"

Serenity took her eyes off of Baxter while looking around at flaming torches along the beach, other couples smiling, dancing and drinking. She heard Baxter's chair then turned her attention back in his direction, behind him stood Tammy. It seemed as if every sound came to a screeching halt. She began to hear piano keys tapping out a familiar song. Tammy opened her mouth and began to sing the most melodic tones Serenity had ever heard. As her eyes bounced from

Baxter to Tammy then she searched for the piano where Jason sat, she didn't notice Baxter kneel in front of her. By the time her head had bounced back his way, her eyes were streaming tears. Baxter took her hand as he looked up into her eyes. When Tammy's singing ceased he began to speak.

"Baby, bear with me, I'm not the most poetic. I had to borrow a few lyrics but I mean every word."

Serenity nodded then he continued.

"If God one day struck me blind, your beauty I'd still see. Love is too weak to define what you mean to me. The first moment I saw you I knew you were the one. I could not see living another day without you in it. I wouldn't want to. That's why until the end of time I'll be there for you. You own my body, my mind and my soul. I truly adore you. I just need to know that you, Serenity Faith Carson will be my wife. Will you allow me to love you until the end time?" He said as he slipped a ring onto her finger.

"Yes! I will marry you," Serenity said as she nodded.

The entire place erupted in applause as Serenity took Baxter into her arms. She kissed him as if they were the only two people there. As the tears were wiped from her face, Baxter took a moment to view her colors. They were nothing he'd ever seen around her before. The bright purples, blues, red and pink seemed to swirl together and dance around her. Baxter was filled with warmth knowing she was completely elated at the time.

****

"Do you know he wouldn't even have sex with me?"

"What do you mean, wouldn't?" Christian asked.

Serenity was on the phone with Christian catching him up on her vacation with Baxter.

"I mean, he wouldn't. I tried and he said no."

"Ummmm? Does he know you offered him a sacred garden?"

"Yes, he knows."

"So, you mean to tell me he didn't want any of that virgin loving?"

"He said he wanted to wait until we were married."

"That's a first. You better check that package. Maybe, he ain't got much to offer."

"No. Baxter wants our wedding night to be extra special is all," Serenity explained.

"I'm just saying."

"Sometimes, you can be so crass."

"Call it what you want but, it's the truth."

"That's not the case. After he proposed things got a little heated when we got back to our hut. I was willing to give him whatever he wanted."

"I would've too. All that romance and ocean and I wish a man would do something like that for me."

"He stopped it, not me. And told me how much he wanted it, how much he knew it was a precious gift to him. But, he wanted my virginity to be his wedding gift."

"Ain't that sweet, he's crazy and you are too. Y'all better figure out if y'all fit before you go jumping the broom."

"Our connection is strong. I don't think we'll have one single problem."

Then she recalled their first kiss, how the sky opened for them, she couldn't wait to see what would happen when they made love.

"When is the planning starting?"

"We won't have anything big. Neither of us have much family, you are my only friend."

"You just set a date, I'll be there. Oh my God! You've got to let me design your gown. I'll be there next week for measurements. My head is spinning thinking about it. I'll bring you some fabric swatches."

"You don't have time for that Christian, I couldn't ask you to do that."

"You didn't ask. What the hell are awesome friends for?"

"You are awesome."

"Honey, tell me something I don't know."

Clayton

"Do you remember when I first told you I was going to ask Serenity to marry me?" Baxter asked Clayton.

"Yeah, I remember," Clayton said as he thought of the day.

"Well, I did it. I asked her," Baxter stated as soon as he walked in his home.

"I assume she said yes by the smile plastered on your face," Clayton stated.

"How could she not? We were meant to be together."

"You keep saying that."

"We have so many things in common. There's nothing we can't share. I can't stand being away from her. We can tell each other anything."

"You mean you told her **everything**?"

"Yes, Clayton. I told her I was touched with colorful sight."

"How'd she take that?"

"Oh my God, she was so receptive. Serenity asks questions, she wants to understand what I see."

"I'm happy for you, man," Clayton said unenthusiastically.

"Yeah, I can really tell. The excitement is radiating from your pores," Baxter stated sarcastically.

"Really, I am. It's just strange. I'm used to being the one holding your secrets. It'll take some getting used to."

"Dude, you don't even like to talk about it."

"I know; I guess I should apologize for that."

"It's not necessary, I completely understand."

Clayton zoned out for a minute remembering how he felt that day. He was happy for his brother but he couldn't help fearing he'd lost his best friend. For so long, Baxter had been the one there for him. Here he was saying he didn't want to settle down now he wondered if that's what he really meant. Clayton had spent so much time trying to avoid becoming attached to anyone. Now, he was contemplating whether or not he was capable.

Baxter brought Clayton back to the present with his constant pacing which he'd begun again.

"Would you sit down?"

"I can't. Isn't it time yet?" Baxter asked as he looked at his watch.

"You can't rush perfection. They'll tell us when to come down. Tell me about when you first met Serenity's father."

Clayton was just trying to distract Baxter and he knew it.

"You don't want to hear about that. You just want me to shut up."

"Well, I'll tell you it shocked the shit out of me when I met him. I mean you could've forewarned me."

"What was I supposed to say?" Baxter asked with a chuckle.

"I don't know. You say 'dude, he's white'."

"Why does it matter?"

"It doesn't matter. I mean, it just wasn't what I expected. I come in looking all over for dude while he was standing in my face."

"She hadn't told me he was white when I went to her house to meet him either. You should've seen my face when I walked in the house."

"It probably looked better than mine. But he's a cool dude."

"He is," Baxter said.

"Did he try to give you any 'take care of my daughter talk'?"

"No. He knows she's in great hands."

"B, you ever wonder…. Never mind."

"Come on, what is it you wonder?"

"I don't want to bring you down or anything but aren't you a little sad today?"

"Why would I be sad? It's my wedding day."

"Well, I'm just thinking how great it would be if mom and dad were here."

"Clay, you know I thought about that but trust me they're here."

"I would have loved for them to meet Serenity, I can see mom trying to fix her hair," he said with a chuckle.

"That would be a disaster," Baxter laughed then noticed the look on his brother's face.

"I mean even the happiest days bring about sad memories."

"Clayton, I'm going to tell you something but you have got to promise not to freak out. You can-not let Serenity know I told you."

Clay looked at his brother with a look of confusion. Baxter continued before he could answer.

"I know our parents are here and they have met Serenity."

"Yeah, I think we need to call this off. I may need to check you into the psych ward."

"I don't even know how to say this to you."

"When have you not just said what it was? You aren't about to say our parents are alive and in witness protection or something are you?"

"No, nothing like that."

"Then what?"

"Serenity can communicate with spirits."

Clayton just looked at him blankly. His mind went a million places then he finally settled on one question.

"Have you talked to them?"

"No. Neither has she, really. She told me she saw mom one day and she can feel them but they haven't come to her."

"Why not?"

"I can't answer that."

"I wasn't asking you. I'm asking them. You said they're here, right? If they have had the opportunity to speak with you why haven't they?"

Baxter could see the anger all around Clayton. He knew Clayton still had not grieved as he should have. Deep down Baxter suspected this grief had a lot to do with his behavior.

"I'm sure they have their reasons."

"I don't see how you just accept what comes, accept the fu---- messed up shit that happens like it's ok."

"Being ok with it is not the issue. Can I do anything about it? Will me stressing over the course of life and circumstances change any one thing? No. I choose to look at the great, good and even just acceptable parts of life. I'd rather not dwell in the past, grief or anger."

"That's easy to say."

"It would be easier for you if you even tried it. I've done it so long I don't know how to look at life any other way. So, you may be right; it's easy for me. I just have faith that everything will be right when all is said and done."

"I hope I get there," Clayton said in a solemn tone.

"Of course, you'll get there."

Baxter walked over and embraced his brother as he prayed his words were true.

"That wasn't the reaction I expected when I told you about Serenity."

"Dude, nothing shocks me anymore. I mean, maybe if you would've told me she was a vampire or something."

"I don't know if it's a good or bad thing."

"It's all good. I put up with your weird cryptic ass. She can't be much worse."

"I'm weird, huh?"

"Dude, you know you're weird. Don't try to pretend to be offended. I love you all the same."

They shared a laugh. Baxter checked his watch.

"It's about that time."

"I'll go check," Clayton said as he reached for the door.

He couldn't wait to get out of that room. The tears behind his eyes were pushing so hard. That wasn't what Baxter needed today. His brother needed a best man not a blubbering mess to comfort. The fact was, Clayton was more hurt than angry. Baxter didn't know Clay talked to his parents at least once daily and had questions that had yet to be answered. He now felt abandoned. Today, wasn't the day for that. He hoped with all hope he could rid himself of this feeling. Before heading down the hall to see if Serenity was ready, he stepped in the restroom.

Clayton looked at himself in the mirror. He saw the tears behind his eyes but refused to let them fall. After dampening a hand towel with cold water and pressing it to his face he headed in his soon-to-be sister in law's direction. When he arrived at Serenity's door, he could've sworn he heard someone talking. He tapped lightly.

"Peace, are you ready?"

"Come in Clayton."

"Are you sure?" He asked as he cracked the door. "No one is supposed to see your dress."

"Your brother isn't supposed to see my dress, you can."

"Are you," Clayton stopped mid-sentence.

"Is something wrong?"

"Not at all. You look hot!"

Serenity blushed.

"Christian did a wonderful job on my dress, didn't he?"

"It's stunning, I had no idea your body was banging like that."

"CLAYTON!"

"I'm sorry. I wasn't saying it in a creepy way. I'm just saying."

"You're a mess."

"I can go tell Bax you're ready. He's about to lose it, pacing the floor and sh—stuff."

Serenity chuckled.

"I'm ready. I'm beyond ready."

"Good. I'll let him know," Clay said as he turned to leave.

"Clayton. I want to tell you something first."

"It can wait Peace," Clayton said.

Hearing him use the name he'd given her made her recall the day they met. Baxter wanted her to meet the person he held nearest to his heart. He'd invited her over for dinner with Clayton and his latest girl toy. They didn't do much talking at dinner. She wasn't sure Clayton took too well to her. Serenity surely knew she wasn't fond of this girl he'd toted along. After dinner they all played a few rounds of dominoes. There they laughed, talked, joked, bantered of politics and etc. It wasn't until Clayton was making his departure that gave Serenity a clue he'd indeed accepted her.

"It was very nice meeting you Ser- you know what? Your name has too many syllables. I'm going to call you Peace."

"Peace, I'll take that. No one has ever attempted to give me a nickname before. I think, I like it."

"Nice meeting you, I'll be seeing you I'm sure," Clayton said before exiting.

Serenity chuckled thinking who counts syllables in names.

"No, Clayton this can't wait. Come in sit next to me for a second."

Serenity took a seat on the small loveseat and patted the cushion next to her. She admired Clayton's stride, it was regal.

"What's up sis? I guess I can't call you that yet, huh? You're not about to tell me you got cold feet, are you? Because Baxter might jump out the window."

"Hush, silly. Of course, I'm not backing out. I want to talk to you."

"Ok, because he is a nervous wreck."

"As much as you're talking I'd say you are too."

"Hey, I'm not getting married."

"Not today but the thought of doing it someday makes you anxious."

"I'm not thinking about that. These shallow women aren't the wife type in my book."

"That's why you pick them. Don't be afraid to love."

"Hey, what is this therapy? We don't have time for all that," Clayton said as he looked at his watch.

"It's my wedding, we have all the time I want. But your love life isn't what I wanted to talk to you about."

"Whew, good."

"Clayton, I know how close you and your brother are. I want you to know that whenever you need him, he'll be there for you. I would never try to get in the way of that. I'm not the type of person that needs to be first in everything all the time."

"It will be an adjustment for me."

"Don't you worry. You can still call him at 4 AM when you need to talk or to pick you up. I don't want you to hesitate. You'll always have a place in his heart, that place hasn't gotten smaller. His heart got bigger to make room for me, not to take away from you."

The tears that threatened Clay's eyes before were back. He wasn't sure he would be able to hold them this time.

"I appreciate you saying that Serenity."

"Whoa, you used all my syllables," Serenity said with a chuckle as she shoved him slightly.

"You got all serious on me. I had to pull the adult Clayton out."

"Clay, there's one more thing."

"Come on Peace. B is going to explode if we don't get this going."

"He'll be alright. I have to say this to you now while I have you here."

They sat there a few seconds, Clayton gazed at the side of Serenity's face. She looked so flawless he wanted to touch her face to see if she was real.

"Peace, are you gonna talk?"

"Yes, it's just hard to say things sometimes."

"Just say it. That's what I do."

"Don't we know you speak your mind."

"Why hold it in?"

"Ok. Here goes," Serenity began with a huge breath.

"Your mother wants you to know she is very proud of you. She doesn't want you to give up on your education. Vivian says she knows sometimes you want to quit but she nudges you to keep going. They have not left you on your own. You will have all the answers to your questions in the right time. Hugh wants you to know there is no rush to find that ONE. She is waiting on you to find her when you're ready but don't be so scared of hurt you'll never love. They are with you every morning when you get in your car. You haven't been left to fend for yourself. You have been pushed to show your strength because you are destined for great things. And even though she wasn't supposed to tell you; you need to know that, in this time. They will never leave you accept at night when you bring those trollops home."

Serenity looked up to see Clayton chuckle at the last statement through his tears. She reached over to hug him and he couldn't help but hold her tight and let the tears go. He'd been holding on to them for so long. The dam burst and it was nothing he could do about it. Serenity held on to him, fighting her own tears. She could feel all sorts of emotions pouring from his soul. It was as if he was unburdening himself from so much.

"Thank you," Clayton finally said as he pulled away.

"I'll be there for you whenever you need."

Serenity handed him tissue from the box next to her.

"These are supposed to be for me. Now, get out of here before you ruin my make-up. Tell my dad I'm ready."

Serenity

It didn't even bother me that Clayton didn't look at me strange or ask a million questions when I told him what his parents said. I know, if Baxter told him, he had his reasons and he must've needed to know. Which is probably why his parents revealed themselves to me. I've felt them around before but it was amplified today. First it was Vivian, then Hugh appeared next to her. She spoke to me softly.

"I don't know how this goes Serenity," Vivian said.

"Ma 'am it goes like any other conversation."

"Are you afraid?"

"Of you? No, I've gotten used to people showing up on me when I least expect."

"I don't mean of us dear girl, at what happens next."

"I'm a nervous wreck!"

"You have no need to be,"

"Though I know that. Somehow, it seems I have so many butterflies floating around in my stomach. I think they want to escape."

"You know I'm not going to say too much but, I will say I'm happy my son found you."

"Thank you Ma'am, that means a lot to me."

"First, let's get this straight. Stop calling me ma'am. I'll take Viv, mom or even Vivian just stop calling me ma'am."

"Yes, m…. Viv. I'm sorry."

"Now, I didn't come here to talk about you and Baxter. You guys will be fine. I need you to get a message to Clayton. Can you help me with that?"

"Of course, I can."

"Whether you know it or not, he's having a hard time with this marriage. He has nothing against you. He's happy for his brother but he's feeling as if he's not sure where that leaves him."

"Baxter would never leave him out."

"He knows that too. But doesn't want to intrude either."

"I love Clayton; he is a character all his own."

"Don't I know it. But honey, that's seriously a mask for his pain. He will have a break through and he will find the other part to his soul, just not right now. I don't want him to give up."

"I wouldn't want him to either."

"You don't know the dark places he goes, sometimes. I just need him to understand that we're here."

"I will tell him."

"Serenity, I'm glad we get to meet you even if no other person knows it."

"That means a lot to me Viv."

"I know it's hard on you too sometimes. Even though, you're used to it. Whenever you feel overwhelmed just call on me. I'll be there to listen. And I know you have others to talk to but if there's ever something, I just want you to know I'm here. I love your spirit. I only wish we could've been able to know you better."

"Viv, cut out all that wishing and just be happy. Don't try to bring the girl down," Hugh said.

"That's not what I'm doing."

"Hell, sounds like it to me," Hugh turned toward Serenity and continued.

"You are a bright light for our family and we love you like we've known you forever. Don't listen to all that down talk Momma is spewing. She's just in her feelings about that youngest one of ours. He'll be fine too. Momma just worries too much. Ain't no need in worrying when we already know what's going on from this side. She just don't know how to do nothing else."

"I'm right here," Viv reminded.

"I know you are. I been listening to you talk, now it's my turn."

Serenity chuckled at the exchange between the two of them and couldn't help but wonder if she and Baxter would be that way one day.

"Hugh, you talk too much."

"Ain't that the pot?"

"Serenity, you have our blessings, let us get out of here so you can get to your big day."

"I would like to ask you a favor, if I can," Serenity stated.

"What is it honey?"

"Later on, tomorrow maybe, will you pay us a visit. I want Baxter to know you're there and to talk to you as my wedding present to him."

"Of course, darling, of course. But let's give y'all a couple days. You got wedding business to take care of," Viv said with a smirk.

Serenity turned red as a beet from embarrassment.

"Ain't nothing to be ashamed of honey, I was a virgin when I married this old geezer. You see he ain't gone nowhere. Death couldn't even do us part," she said and began to chuckle.

"You know you ain't funny, Vivian," Hugh said with a disappointing look.

"You don't think anything is funny, Hugh. Come on here, let them go get hitched."

And with that, they faded away. Serenity couldn't help but smile at herself in the mirror thinking how she would enjoy having them around.

Just then her father knocked on the door.

"Come in daddy, I'm ready."

Her father entered the room, his eyes filled with tears as soon as they focused upon her.

"You look like an angel."

"Thank you, daddy."

"Are you ready?"

"Absolutely," she said as she beamed with joy.

Harold extended his elbow, just as Serenity interlaced hers he spoke,

"I wish your momma was here to see you, now. If I could go back to stop that drunk driver that ran that car off the road, I'd step in front of it myself. I'm glad God spared me you to allow you to come and take care of me."

"Daddy, don't you worry about momma being here, she is. She has always been with me. She wouldn't trust me with you," Serenity said with a chuckle.

"I suppose you're right," Harold answer with his own sad laugh.

"Come on daddy, it's time for me to go take care of someone else. I'll always be around to look after you. You aren't losing me."

"I know, Smooch, I know."

With those words, they exited the small room heading toward the sanctuary of the church. Just as Serenity exited the room she turned to look in the mirror where she saw her mom, aunt Lillie and Mammie in the mirror smiling and nodding their heads in agreement.

Harold

As Harold anxiously awaited his honor of escorting his daughter down the aisle, his mind couldn't help but to travel back in time. Remembering her childhood, which ultimately caused him to think about the love of his life and the biggest mistake he ever made.

Harold and Lydia met in a time when it wasn't the best idea for the two to date. In the beginning, that was the draw for him. He was always one to push the limits. He hung out on the wrong side of town and was revered as the black sheep in his family. When he met Lydia, he had lots of women. It took some time convincing Lydia to go out with him. She was on the straight and narrow and saw him as a world of trouble. He set out to prove her wrong.

Lydia worked the counter at the local store, he showed up every day for a week with flowers and candy just for her. She'd finally agreed to let him take her to lunch, that's when Harold knew he'd won her over. From that day forward they spent time together, every day. When his dance started with Lydia it was more of him winning a challenge than it was of winning her heart. Something happened to Harold along the way, Lydia captured his heart. That meant everything to Harold.

But when all was said and done, Harold was a coward. When his father found out about Lydia he made him choose between family money and the love of his life. Of all the things Harold did, standing up to his father was something that had never happened. In a way, being a black sheep was his best way to get back at his dad for the reigns he opposed on him. But this was one his dad would not let loose of. For Harold Sr. it was not proper for the son of the mayor to run around with a girl from the wrong side of the tracks.

He wore shame all over him, too ashamed to tell Lydia the truth. So, he figured the best thing to do was to make her hate him. When he didn't show up at the store one day, Lydia came looking for him at one of his regular haunts. He knew she would, that's why he picked that day to take a bite of the flirts the regular barmaid threw his way. By the time Lydia showed up, Harold was drunk. Brandi was sitting in his lap and he pretended not to see Lydia when he kissed Brandi. As soon as Lydia ran out crying, Harold felt his lowest. He immediately pushed Brandi from his lap. It killed him to cause Lydia so much pain. But, he feared what his father would do if he didn't let her go.

Harold couldn't bare being so close to Lydia but being unable to be with her. He went to his father under the guise of becoming a responsible adult, wanting to start his own business not under the thumb of Sr. He would venture off to another town, far away from Lydia. Harold thought it would be easier for Lydia to hate him from afar. And so, he set off to live in another town to have a better time, to give Lydia a better life without him.

Serenity was five when Harold came into town for Sr's 70th birthday party. As he drove through the center of town, he caught sight of Lydia from the corner of his eye. He'd know her anywhere. Harold contemplated stopping to speak but when he saw there was a tiny hand in hers, he thought better of it. He hadn't realized he stopped in the middle of the street until someone yelled at him to move. The commotion not only got his attention but Lydia's also. When she looked up, their eyes met. He looked with questioning eyes. She looked with contempt. Lydia was the first to break their stare. She rushed along with a little girl in tow.

Harold hadn't known Lydia was pregnant when he left. She never tried to contact him either.

How could she not tell me?

For Harold, that made everything different. He would've stood up to his father for their child. How could his father not tell him? For that, he would never forgive him. That week, Harold couldn't get Lydia off his mind. He wanted to reach out to her but he knew she would never speak to him. He wore shame all over his body.

He knew then no matter what his father felt, he had to make it right. Even if Lydia wouldn't have him, he would not forsake his daughter.

Baxter

As soon as he saw Serenity grace the threshold of the sanctuary, tears filled his eyes. Her aura nearly blinded him. She was the most beautiful thing he'd ever seen. Baxter couldn't believe she was there to be his for life. With each step, she seemed to sparkled. He could see their future. He saw the day she gives birth. Which made him anxious for their wedding night. Baxter shook that thought from his head, feeling sinful because his mind filled with sex standing in church. The closer she got, the harder it became to hold back his tears.

Baxter watched as her narrow hips swayed as she walked. Serenity became brighter and brighter the closer she got to him. The dress hung on her as if she'd grown it herself. The champagne gold was perfect against her skin and the rhinestones on her bodice matched the sparkle in her eyes. The rainbow-colored bouquet was just right for her glow.

Serenity stood at the foot of the alter with her eyes sparkling like diamonds. Baxter was nearly dancing in place waiting for the officiant to say it was his time to retrieve his wife from where she stood. Her smile looked like the sun to him.

"Who gives this woman?" The officiant asked.

"I do," her father stated.

Baxter made his way down the three steps that separated them, touched her hand to lead her back. The sky opened up. Serenity looked to the sky then back at the crowd behind them, back to Baxter. It seemed none of them could see what they could. The light of the sun seemed to light their way as if it were a spot light from the heavens making sure they were seen.

"You are an angel," Baxter told her.

Serenity blushed, she was scared to speak. Her tears threatened to fall and nearly escaped when she saw Baxter's waterfall streaming his cheeks. She could see the pride on his face. She could see the love in his eyes.

The officiant began speaking and Baxter wasn't hearing a word. He was lost in Serenity's eyes. He looked deeply at the rainbows that shimmered in her soul. For the first time on this day he felt at ease. He knew she was for him; she was just as happy to be his as he was to be hers. In that moment, he let out a deep breath, all his worries went with it.

Serenity

Serenity was a ball of nerves when the doors to the sanctuary opened up. It was like her entire life stood before her.

"It's ok, honey," her father said.

She felt him squeeze her hand as they started down the aisle. That gesture put her at ease. Serenity's face lit up as she looked up the aisle and could see a glow surround Baxter. He was her future; he was her everything. There he stood waiting for her, to be hers. Her heart filled with joy, she saw the future flash before her. Serenity beamed as she saw both their parents standing at the alter smiling, waiting for them to become family.

Now, she stood looking in Baxter's eyes, ready to recite the vows she'd written. She barely heard what came before, she wanted to tell him all she felt from the moment she'd met him. As Baxter began to say the vows he'd prepared she tuned in.

"The moment I saw you, you lit up my life. I knew that no one would ever look or feel the same to me. There was no way I could let you slip through my fingers. I'm glad I got a hold of you. I vow to never let you go, to cherish you, protect you, support you and love you until there is no life in me left and beyond."

Serenity could see the tears pool in Baxter's eyes. She took a deep breath before she declared her love for him to the world.

"Baxter, you walked into my life and my entire world changed. When I first laid eyes on you, everything about you was different. And I embrace you and all the things about you. I love you for accepting my quirks, my idiosyncrasies, my ups and downs. I vow to love you, support you, build with you, grow with you, adapt to your changes as you adapt to mine. I have loved you all my life without even knowing you and I promise to continue to do so in this world and the next."

The officiant continued with a prayer and other rhetoric. Serenity was waiting for this part.

"I now pronounce you man and wife. You may kiss the bride."

Serenity leaned in to kiss Baxter and just as she expected the light was blinding. She closed her eyes and chuckled a bit into Baxter's lips. She wondered for a second if anyone else could see what she sees. Just when she pulled away, Baxter whispered to her.

"I can see them," he looked her in the eye with a huge smile.

They turned together to be presented to the audience. Serenity was blinded by a rainbow of colors.

"Is that what it looks like?" Serenity said in a hushed tone.

They marched down the aisle full of smiles. Baxter watched his parents glow with pride and his tears began to fall.

Baxter

Seeing my parents at our wedding, smiling and happy was unbelievable for me. Our wedding night was nothing less than earth shattering. Just as before when we kissed, a light shown down on us like we were being anointed from the heavens. And though it was not my first time, unlike Serenity, it surely felt as though it were. I had never felt so deeply. If it had been possible I would have sworn Serenity bore passion at its creation. The lights and colors circled the room.

It felt as if I'd waited all my life to live within her. Ever sense, I had amplified, immensely. I could hear everything in the room, including Serenity's thoughts. You couldn't have told me, I wasn't able to see through to her soul. The air around us was electric. When we climaxed, the earth shook. I do mean literally, we caused an earthquake.

At first, we thought it was just us. That we rumbled each other's souls. We laid there laughing thinking it was only us feeling the bed shake before we drifted off to sleep. When we awoke the next morning, the joke was on us. It was reported as a 4.2 quake. We looked at one another in awe. Not sure of what to think of it. It did not stop us from making love over and over again. We didn't show our faces to the light of day for nearly three days. We shared every inch of our bodies with one another.

I never would've expected that when I became one with Serenity that we would literally share everything. We had to teach one another to cope with each other's gifts. It's amazing being able to actually see my parents and talk to them. I was ecstatic when I was able to meet Serenity's mom. Ms. Lydia is so serene. I see where Serenity inherited her beautiful soul. It took me a while to understand the signs and warnings that came with her gift. But for her, coping with the many emotions and feelings that came with mine was even more of a challenge. It seemed, I felt things much more deeply now. We share a soul as if our two halves were always part of a whole.

Kaylynn on Amazon

A Detroit native, Kaylynn grew up on the east side of the city and has always had an insatiable passion for writing. She graduated from Detroit Public Schools. Kaylynn began her family early; she was married at the age of 23. She chose to show her three sons that it's never too late to follow your dreams.

Kaylynn is not easily influenced by the 'norm' and it comes across on her pages by challenging the conventional. Kaylynn produces captivating and stimulating pieces of work, which absorb the reader down to the last page. Kaylynn has used not only her imagination, but glimpses of the life she's lived, in order to produce quality, flowing works of art.

Living outside the box is something she excels at. She believes that the mind is one of our most wonderful assets here on earth. Kaylynn opens you up to things that will make you think outside the box. Her hope is that through her stimulating roller coaster rides of emotion; your mind will have the proper exercise necessary for continued growth and enlightenment.

Want to read more of this author, find more titles on Amazon, visit her webpage: www.KaylynnHunt.com.

Made in the USA
Monee, IL
08 March 2023